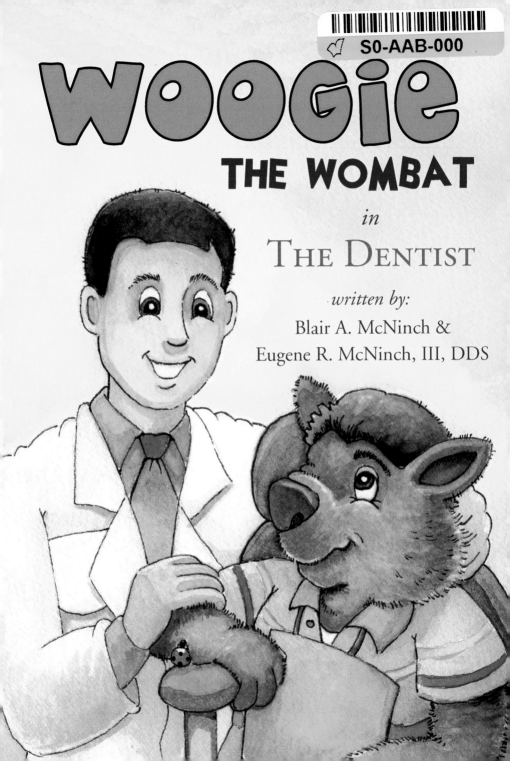

WOOGIE
THE WOMBAT

in

THE DENTIST

written by:

Blair A. McNinch &
Eugene R. McNinch, III, DDS

Published by Tate Publishing & Enterprises, LLC
127 E. Trade Center Terrace | Mustang, Oklahoma 73064 USA
1.888.361.9473 | www.tatepublishing.com

Tate Publishing is committed to excellence in the publishing industry. The company reflects the philosophy established by the founders, based on Psalm 68:11,
"The Lord gave the word and great was the company of those who published it."

Book design copyright © 2008 by Tate Publishing, LLC. All rights reserved.
Cover design & interior design by Elizabeth A. Mason
Illustrations by Jason Hutton

Published in the United States of America

ISBN: 978-1-60696-355-5
1. Juvenile Fiction: Animals: Wombats
2. Youth & Children: Children: Animals
08.07.10

In loving memory of Blair A. McNinch

Special thanks to Michael Houk, Blair's
inspiring U.S. Army buddies, my loving wife
Abigail, Sarah Maisel, and Mark Palmer

"Hi! I'm Sweeney the Zookeeper. I take care of all of the zoo animals and this is my very special friend, Woogie. Woogie is a wombat from Australia. Wombats are like you and me—cute, curious, and friendly! They enjoy rooting for food and trundling about. Just look at Woogie trundle! Woogie is getting ready for his first trip to the dentist."

"The dentist?" Woogie asked. "Why do I have to see the dentist?"

"Visiting the dentist is important for a healthy wombat. How can you root properly without strong teeth? Dentists help to make sure that your teeth are nice and strong," said Zookeeper Sweeney.

Woogie, very nervous, ran to the burrows. He didn't know what to expect on his visit to the dentist, so he decided to use the burrows around the zoo to ask his friends about the dentist.

At the closest burrow, he met Aru the Alligator.

"Hello, Aru," said Woogie. "Do you know anything about somebody called a dentist?" Now keep in mind, Aru was a nice alligator, but he was also tricky and liked to play jokes sometimes.

"You're going to the dentist, Woogie?" questioned Aru. "I went there once. I used to have one hundred teeth, but after the dentist I only had fifty! And just look at what he did to my spines." Aru laughed, but Woogie was still nervous and decided to move on.

Woogie found Slew the Kangaroo and Monifa the Mole chatting by the watering hole. "Hi, Slew! Hi, Monifa!" greeted Woogie. "I have to go to the dentist soon. I think that I'm scared!" exclaimed Woogie, nervously.

"Don't be scared, Woogie," they both said at once. "I've had my teeth cleaned three times, Woogie," said Slew. "I got a toy or sticker every time!"

"Yeah," said Monifa. "I use my teeth a lot, and the dentist always makes sure that they stay strong and healthy. I haven't chipped a tooth yet!"

"Thanks, mates," said Woogie as he moved on.

Trundling further through the zoo, Woogie then saw Mortimer the Moose. "Hi, Mortimer," said Woogie.

"Hey, Woogie. I heard from Aru the Alligator that you are going to the dentist. Aru likes to play jokes a lot, Woogie," Mortimer explained. " Don't listen to that joker, eh?"

"Once I had a cavity that hurt so much I couldn't chew my branches like I used to. It hurt wicked bad, ya' know?" Mortimer said.

"Anyway, Woogie, the dentist was very nice and fixed my tooth so that there was no more cavity. Now I can chew branches all I want!"

"Thanks, Mortimer," said Woogie. "I've got to go with Zookeeper Sweeney now to my appointment with the dentist."

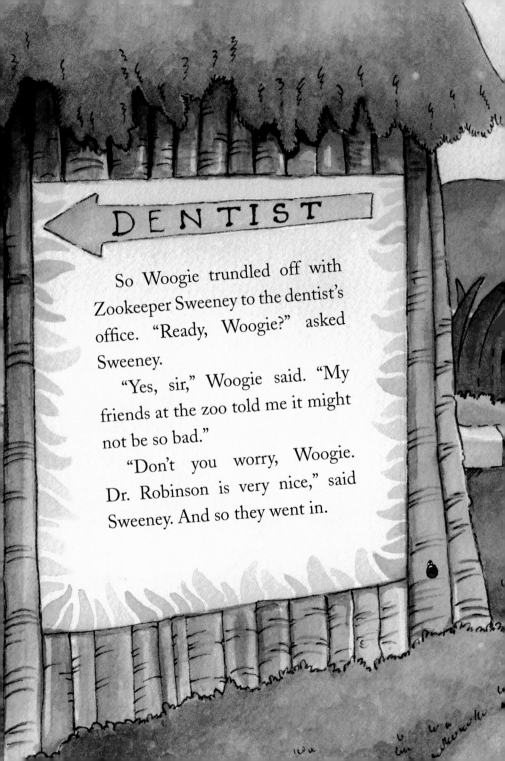

DENTIST

So Woogie trundled off with Zookeeper Sweeney to the dentist's office. "Ready, Woogie?" asked Sweeney.

"Yes, sir," Woogie said. "My friends at the zoo told me it might not be so bad."

"Don't you worry, Woogie. Dr. Robinson is very nice," said Sweeney. And so they went in.

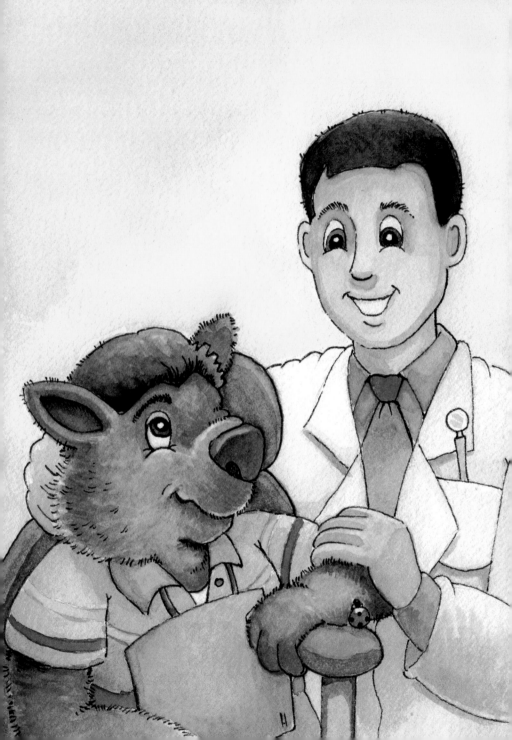

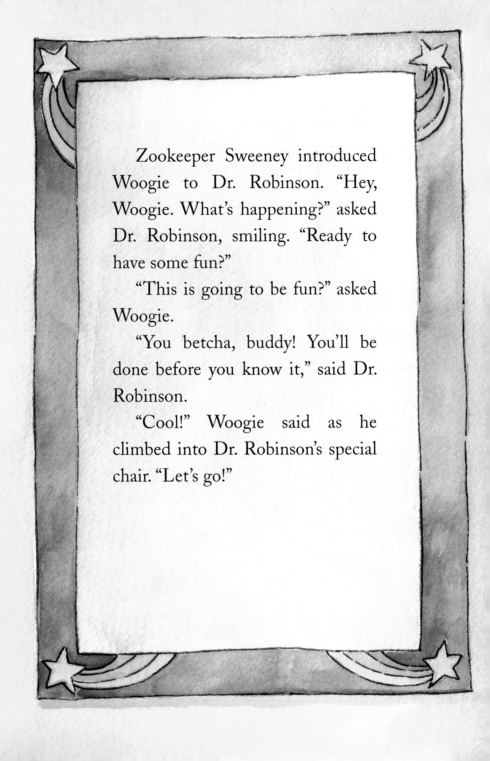

Zookeeper Sweeney introduced Woogie to Dr. Robinson. "Hey, Woogie. What's happening?" asked Dr. Robinson, smiling. "Ready to have some fun?"

"This is going to be fun?" asked Woogie.

"You betcha, buddy! You'll be done before you know it," said Dr. Robinson.

"Cool!" Woogie said as he climbed into Dr. Robinson's special chair. "Let's go!"

"Let's meet our helpers," said Dr. Robinson. "Here's my special tooth mirror and cavity critter finder." Dr. Robinson asked Woogie to open wide. "It looks like some critters have made a cavity, Woogie. Not to worry—this is my cavity critter chaser. It has a headlight and squirts water."

Neat, thought Woogie.

"Now, there's a lot of water, so we also need our friend Mr. Thirsty. He's thirsty for water and cavity critters," explained Dr. Robinson. "Great job keeping your mouth open wide like an alligator! We chased away all of the cavity critters."

"My friend Aru taught me how to open wide," boasted a smiling Woogie.

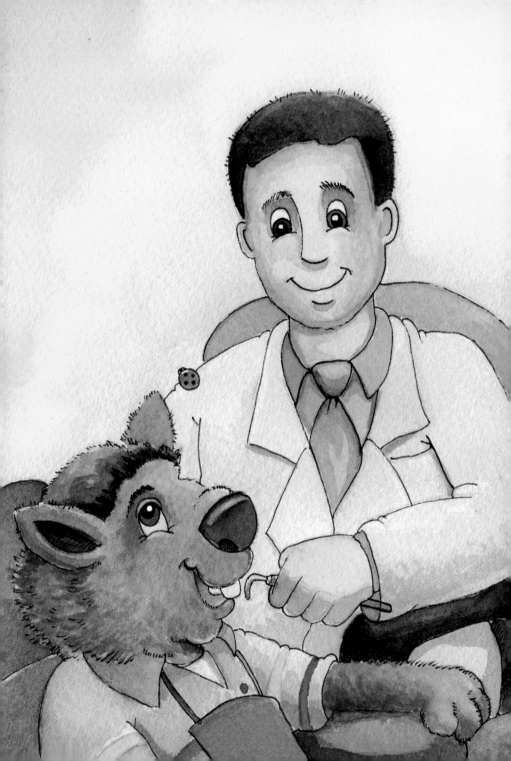

"Now it's time to fill in the hole where those naughty cavity critters were. That way no other cavity critters will try to climb back in your tooth," advised Dr. Robinson.

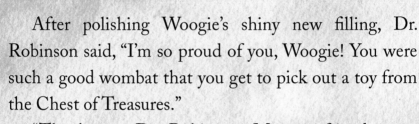

After polishing Woogie's shiny new filling, Dr. Robinson said, "I'm so proud of you, Woogie! You were such a good wombat that you get to pick out a toy from the Chest of Treasures."

"Thank you, Dr. Robinson. My zoo friends were right—it is fun going to the dentist!" said a very happy little Woogie the Wombat.

e|LIVE

listen|imagine|view|experience

AUDIO BOOK DOWNLOAD INCLUDED WITH THIS BOOK!

In your hands you hold a complete digital entertainment package. Besides purchasing the paper version of this book, this book includes a free download of the audio version of this book. Simply use the code listed below when visiting our website. Once downloaded to your computer, you can listen to the book through your computer's speakers, burn it to an audio CD or save the file to your portable music device (such as Apple's popular iPod) and listen on the go!

How to get your free audio book digital download:

1. Visit www.tatepublishing.com and click on the e|LIVE logo on the home page.
2. Enter the following coupon code:
   554d-5af3-03bb-ede6-5bc8-5aac-8f32-2341
3. Download the audio book from your e|LIVE digital locker and begin enjoying your new digital entertainment package today!